Hi. I'm Cecil.

Kumusta. Ako si Cecil.

An elephant is in my room!

May elepante sa kuwarto ko.

I can't get it out.

Hindi ko ito mailabas.

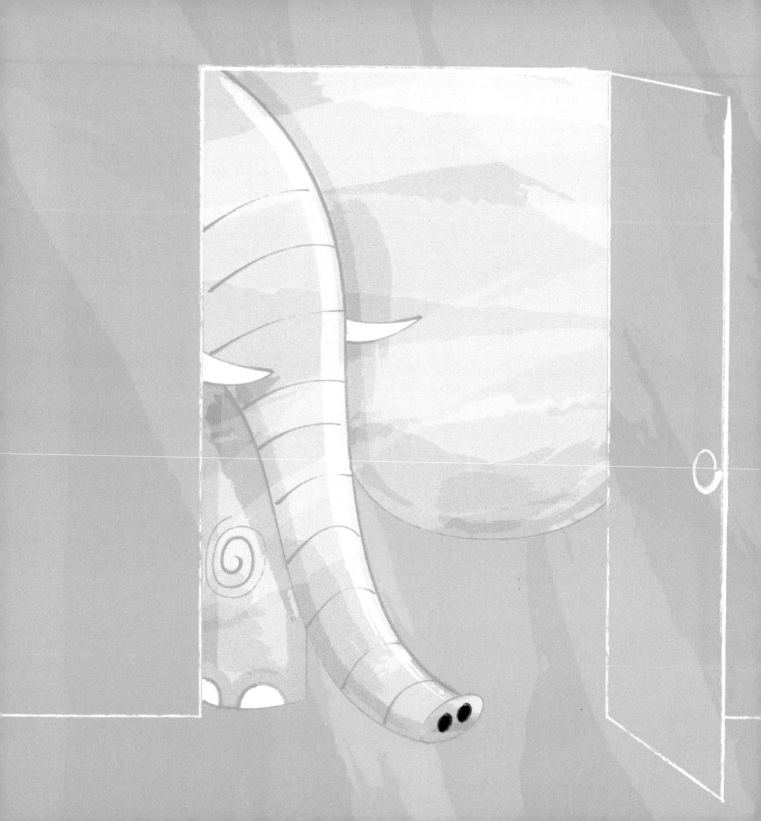

It won't fit through the door.

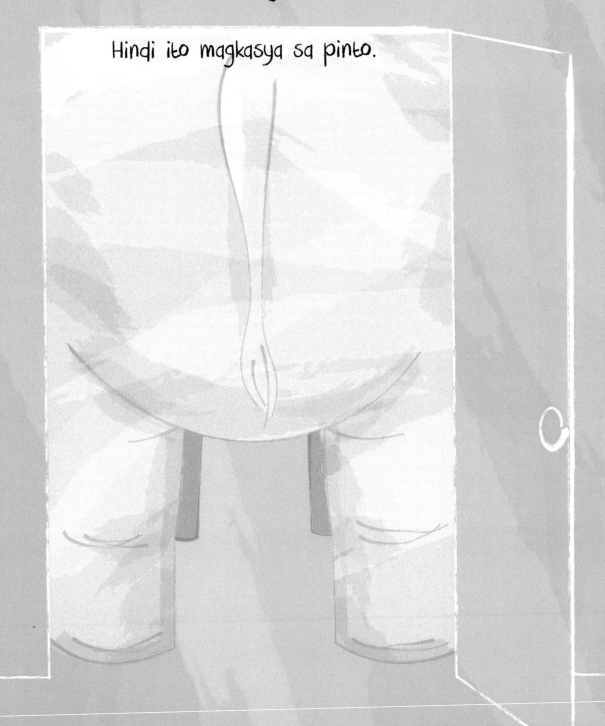

Hindi ito magkasya sa pinto.

It can't squeeze through the window.

Hindi ito maisiksik palabas ng bintana.

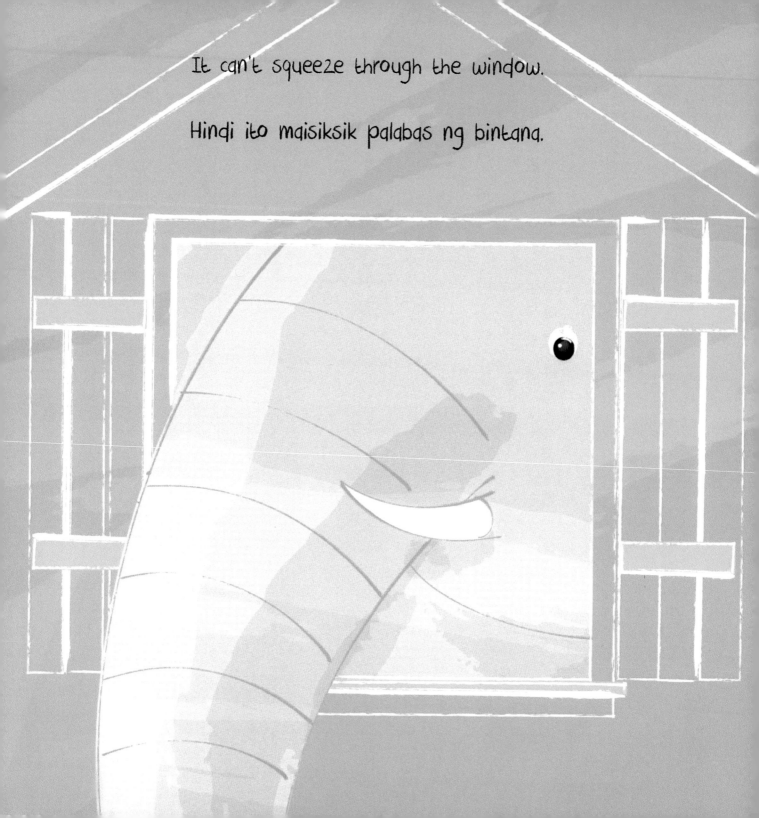

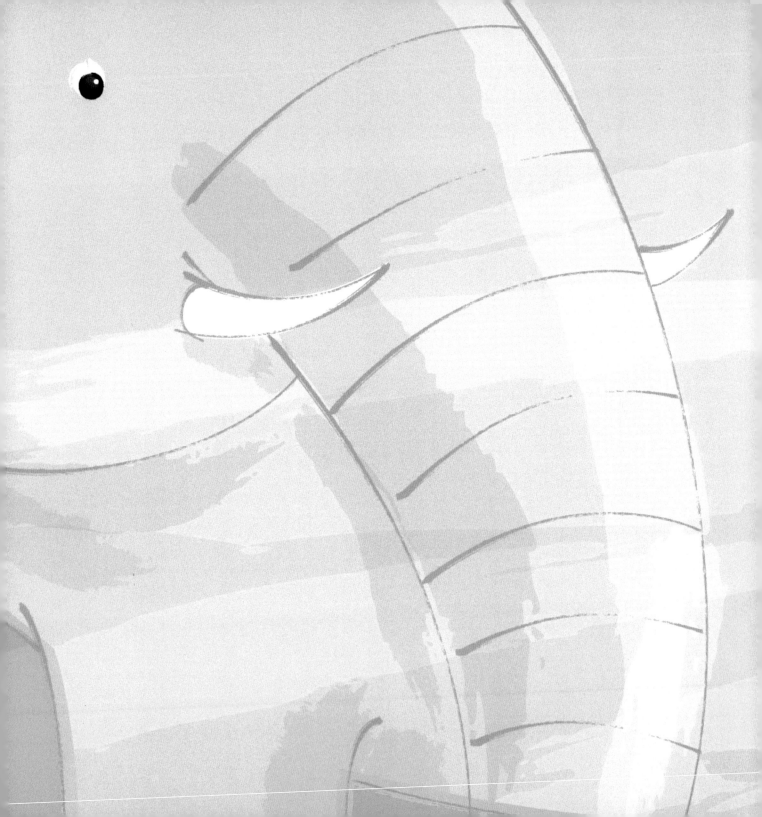

This is a BIG problem.

MALAKING problema ito.

It blocks my closet.

Nakaharang ito sa aking aparador.

Move!

Usod!

It sits on my bed.

Nakaupo ito sa kama ko.

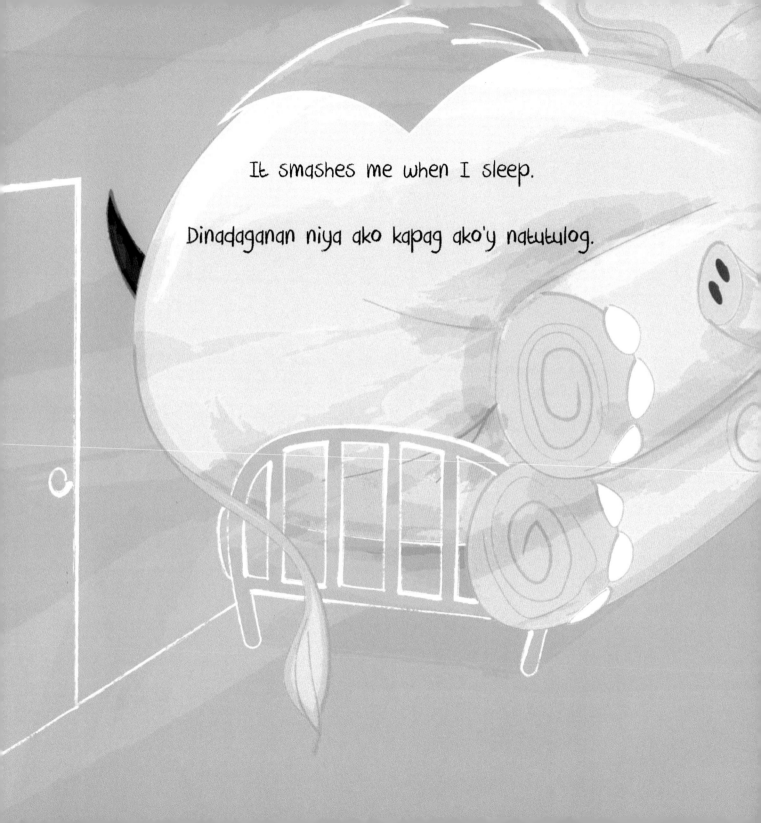

It smashes me when I sleep.

Dinadaganan niya ako kapag ako'y natutulog.

It stares at me.

Tinititigan niya ako.

What if someone finds it?

Paano kung may makakita sa kanya?

No
elifunts

Clara will yell.

Sisigaw si Clara.

Clancy will laugh.

Tatawa si Clancy.

What?!

HA HA
HA HA!

Mom will cry.

Iiyak si Nanay.

No!

Dad will be mad.

Magagalit si Tatay.

I can't leave the house.

Hindi ako makaalis ng bahay.

Someone might find it.

Baka may makakita sa kanya.

I don't know what to do.

Hindi ko alam kung ano ang gagawin ko.

Are you sure?

Sigurado ka?

An elephant is in my room!

May isang elepante sa kuwarto ko!

Oh Cecil. An elephant in your room is a problem.

Naku Cecil. Problema nga ang elepante sa kuwarto mo.

But we can work it out.

Pero magagawan natin ng paraan yan.

If you pretend it's not there, it just gets bigger.

Kung magpapanggap ka na wala ito, lalo itong lalaki.

We can always talk about it.

Pwede naman natin itong pag-usapan.

I love you, Cecil.

Mahal kita, Cecil.

The Elephant In My Room was written specifically to be an instrument to help children with cancer, or children who have a loved one with cancer. The primary goal is to help them to share their feelings, ask questions, and express their fears to a parent, caregiver, or therapist. It is a simple story that illustrates to a child that they are not alone and by sharing their concerns they can find comfort and reassurance. Once a child's fears and uncertainties are known, a parent or care provider can begin to gently and lovingly help the child work through and overcome their challenges.

The general nature of the story also enables it to be a potential tool for helping children with other illnesses as well as physical, social, or emotional challenges.

Grateful acknowledgement is made to Dr. Christopher Lee for his medical expertise, professional input, and his desire to improve communication channels for children impacted by cancer.

The Elephant In My Room
Published by Provenir Publishing, LLC
© 2014 by Micah Harman, all rights reserved.
www.provenirpublishing.com

Provenir
Publishing

Translations made possible by Babl Books Inc.

www.bablbooks.com

Made in United States
Orlando, FL
03 September 2022

21931689R00027